THE
NGUYEN KIDS

The Secret of the
JADE BANGLE

written by
Linda Trinh

illustrated by
Clayton Nguyen

**annick
press**
toronto • berkeley

Cover art by Clayton Nguyen, designed by Paul Covello
Interior designed by Paul Covello and Aldo Fierro
Edited by Katie Hearn
Copy edited by Eleanor Gasparik
Proofread by Mary Ann Blair

Annick Press Ltd.

We acknowledge the support of the Canada Council for the Arts and the
Ontario Arts Council, and the participation of the Government of Canada/
la participation du gouvernement du Canada for our publishing activities.

ONTARIO ARTS COUNCIL
CONSEIL DES ARTS DE L'ONTARIO
an Ontario government agency
un organisme du gouvernement de l'Ontario

Library and Archives Canada Cataloguing in Publication

Title: The secret of the jade bangle / written by Linda Trinh ; illustrated by Clayton Nguyen.
Names: Trinh, Linda, author. | Nguyen, Clayton, illustrator.
Description: "The Nguyen kids"--Cover.
Identifiers: Canadiana (print) 20220167915 | Canadiana (ebook) 2022016794X | ISBN 9781773217154
(hardcover) | ISBN 9781773217161 (softcover) | ISBN 9781773217192 (PDF) | ISBN 9781773217178
(HTML)
Classification: LCC PS8639.R575 S43 2022 | DDC jC813/.6—dc23

Published in the U.S.A. by Annick Press (U.S.) Ltd.
Distributed in Canada by University of Toronto Press.
Distributed in the U.S.A. by Publishers Group West.

Printed in Canada

annickpress.com
lindaytrinh.com
claytonnguyen.art

Also available as an e-book. Please visit annickpress.com/ebooks for more details.

For Lexi and Evan—your stories matter.
—L.T.

To my family.
—C.N.

TABLE OF CONTENTS

CHAPTER 1

Family Ghosts

I, Anne Nguyen, believe in ghosts. Not the kind of ghosts that hide in dark corners and yell *boo!* Not scary ghosts, but family ghosts.

Dad and Mom say we Vietnamese believe the spirits of our family, our ancestors, stay with us after they pass away. They hear our prayers. They watch out for us.

My Grandma Nội died in early spring but we still remember her. Today is the new moon, the day each month we make offerings on her altar. It's my job as the eldest child (I'm nine!) to clean the altar set up in our dining room. As I wipe down the framed picture of Grandma Nội's smiling face, I smile. I look forward to offering days. They make me feel closer to her.

On the altar, there are three ceramic bowls of jasmine rice, three cups of black tea, barbecue pork, kale salad, lasagna, apples, and oranges. We invite the ancestors to share in our meal.

My seven-year-old sister Elizabeth brings out the chopsticks and I line them up neatly next to the bowls.

"You're super helpful, Liz. Thanks!"

She grins at me. Attention makes her light up.

"I miss her," Liz whispers.

I hug Liz. "Me too."

Grandma Nội came to all my ballet shows. She brought my favorite flowers, pink carnations. She slipped me guava candies when Mom and Dad weren't looking.

I loved when she put both her hands on my face. The green jade bangle she wore was cold and smooth along my chin.

Mom sets out chocolate chip cookies on the altar. "We are ready."

I rearrange the cookie platter. Everyone in my family knows I like things super nice and neat.

I look over at my six-year-old brother playing on the couch. "Jacob, no more messes. We're having dinner soon."

"Not yet! Grandma Nội eats first," he replies without looking up from his small building blocks.

I shake my head. Jacob may be spoiled as the baby of the family, but he pays attention.

Dad takes out five joss sticks, long and skinny incense, and lights them. He hands one to each of us—me, Liz, Jacob, and Mom.

Dad closes his eyes. He begins to whisper his prayers, like the rest of the family. It sounds half English and half Vietnamese. I only know a few Vietnamese words.

I hold the joss stick with both hands and close

my eyes. I cough as the flowery smell fills my nose and reaches down my throat.

I say very softly, "Hi, Grandma Nội. It's me, Anne. We went on vacation to Vancouver to visit Mom's family. I can't believe grade four starts in a couple weeks. Mrs. Smith's invitation-only ballet class starts the middle of September too! This is going to be a super-great year. I miss you."

CHAPTER 2
Red Velvet Box

The day before school starts, Liz, Jacob, and I are over at Auntie Hai's house. We help her and my cousins Hanh and Hao clean up their yard. The sun is super warm. At least there are no more mosquitoes now, always annoying in Winnipeg.

I'm in the kitchen to get water for everyone.

I run my hand along the counter and remember Grandma Nội standing at the stove frying my favorite chả giò spring rolls. We spent a lot of time here together. There's an ache in my chest.

Auntie Hai walks in. "Everything okay?"

I nod.

"Thinking about Bà Nội?" she asks.

That's how to say "your dad's mom" in Vietnamese. I nod again, tears sitting at the corners of my eyes.

Grandma and Grandpa Nội always lived with Auntie Hai, Dad's older sister. They live a few blocks away from us. Grandpa Nội lives here still and is taking a nap now.

"We didn't see her in the hospital," I say. I

remember crying on Dad's shoulder when he told us she died.

"She was very sick, and her hair fell out," Auntie Hai reminds me. "We have the altar. Still with us."

Auntie Hai helped us set up our altar like the one at her house. Auntie knows more about Vietnamese stuff than Dad and Mom do. She was born in Vietnam. Both Mom and Dad were born here, in Canada.

Auntie takes my hand. "Call all the other kids in. Have something for you."

Grandpa Nội joins us all in the living room. Auntie opens the shoebox she's holding, and we peer inside.

"Cool. Bà Nội's stuff," Hao says.

Auntie Hai smiles. "Was saving these. Think she would want you to have them. Hanh, as the oldest, her necklace."

Hanh, my 15-year-old cousin, takes the gold chain and gold pendant of the Buddha sitting on a lotus. She squeals.

"Anne," Auntie Hai says, handing me a red velvet box.

"Cám ơn, Auntie," I say, and open the box after thanking her. I got Grandma Nội's green jade bangle! I clasp the box to my heart and feel a warm glow.

Hao, who is the same age as me, gets her fountain pen, and he nods his head.

Liz gets her pearl earrings. She gazes at the

other gifts, trying to decide if we all got better gifts than she did.

And Jacob gets her blue silk fan. "Grandpa, look." He moves to sit next to Grandpa Nội and together they look at the painted animals of the Vietnamese zodiac on the fan.

At home that night before getting into bed, I open the red velvet box and carefully put on the jade bangle. I think of Grandma Nội. I think of her scent of herbal medicine, her warm hands, and her big laugh.

I hear a sound like wind whistling through trees. I feel her with me.

Grandma Nội appears and looks directly at me. "Anne, I need your help!"

CHAPTER 3
Me, Why Me?

"Grandma Nội? Is that you?" I ask. Do I dare to hope?

I can see her, but she is blurry. She is like a reflection in water.

I feel both her hands on my face. Like she used to do. "Cháu yêu quý. Precious granddaughter," she whispers.

"It *is* you! Why haven't you appeared like this to me before?" I ask.

"That's not important. I'm here now. Keep the bracelet safe and wear it when you need me," she says.

I nod. "Yes, Grandma Nội. Do you visit others in the family? Dad? And Auntie Hai?"

She smiles and shrugs her shoulders. "That's between me and them. It's not for you to know. Just like what happens between us is not for others to know. I hear all your prayers. I'm happy you are excited for school and ballet to start. Remember to work hard," she says.

"Yes, Grandma Nội," I whisper, beginning to smile. Her care, her love, it feels so familiar.

"Granddaughter, I need your help. I'm not pleased, and the rest of the ancestors are not either. We're not happy with the food your parents offer us. Why lasagna? Why salad? What about phở, bánh xèo, bò kho! I may be dead, but I still enjoy a nice meal!" She laughs.

I giggle. I forgot how super funny Grandma can be sometimes. "They're always busy."

"Convince them to prepare the food from our homeland," she says.

"But they don't cook a lot of Vietnamese food. You made us phở," I reply.

She nods slowly. "I didn't have the time to teach your dad how to make phở or other foods. I was busy working."

We are both silent for a while.

"So, what happens if the ancestors aren't happy?" I ask.

"They won't grant you good fortune. You must keep the harmony within the family. It's very important."

I play with the jade bangle around my wrist.

"I know!" Grandma Nội's eyes crinkle at the corners. "I will teach you to cook Vietnamese food." She looks pleased with her plan.

"Me? Why me?" I ask. "Why not Hanh? She's the eldest."

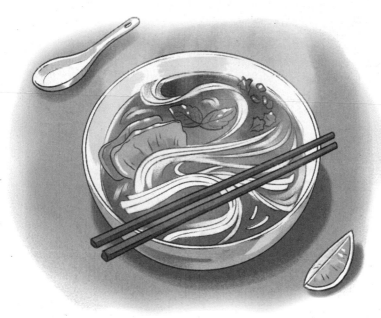

"Precious granddaughter, you followed me around the kitchen. You have the curiosity and attention to do this. It's you I choose," she says, and I feel her hands holding mine.

I want to say yes. I want to make Grandma Nội happy and keep her with me. But I'm scared. What if I can't cook? What if I disappoint her?

CHAPTER 4
First Ballet Class

Waiting for our first ballet class of the year to start, my friend Sophie and I sit on the floor at the dance studio. But I'm still super distracted about what Grandma Nội asked of me. I haven't told anyone. Mom and Dad would expect me to help, of course.

There are nine girls here, including Jennifer Arnason. We compete for everything, at ballet and at school. We are *not* friends. I smile at Jennifer, but like always, she looks away.

When Mrs. Smith walks into the room, I stand up. She's so elegant, with her pale skin, neat blonde bun, and blue eyes. We all had to try out and be invited to this class. Older students say she's tough, but she's been around forever. I'll have to impress her to get a solo part, which is what I want more than anything.

I love ballet. I love the control I have over my body. When I dance, I see my mom's proud face. Mom says she wanted to be a prima ballerina. Her family didn't have enough money for classes. Mom and Dad remind me they work hard now to pay for all our activities.

"Hello, class. Space yourselves at the barre. And stretch," Mrs. Smith says.

Sophie and I line up together.

Mrs. Smith comes toward us.

"Hello. What's your name?" Mrs. Smith asks.

"Sophie Manelli," my friend responds.

"Hello, Sophie. I like your hair," Mrs. Smith says warmly.

She moves to me. "And your name?"

"Anne Nguyen," I say. My voice shakes a little.

"Hi, Anne. Where are you from?" Mrs. Smith asks.

I say right away, "Here. I don't live far away."

She laughs a bit. "No, darling. Where are you really from?" she asks again.

My cheeks begin to feel hot. Oh, *that's* what she means. "Ummm, my parents are from Vietnam and I'm from here."

"Oh, you're from Vietnam," she declares.

"I was born in Winnipeg," I say, unsure of why she asked this question. Why do I feel like I did something wrong?

She smiles and moves on.

Butterflies dance around in my tummy.

I watch. Mrs. Smith doesn't ask anyone else where they are from. I'm the only Asian person here. Everyone except me is white. How did I not notice before?

"She talked to you for so long, Anne. You're lucky!" Sophie whispers to me at the end of class.

"I guess so," I say.

Jennifer shoots me a nasty look as she leaves.

"Even Jennifer is jealous," Sophie continues.

Mrs. Smith did pay extra attention to me. But why do I feel a little confused and a little sad?

My mind goes to Grandma Nội. She said to put on the jade bangle if I needed her. Well, I need her to help me figure out what just happened. I need to help her too. I decide I will cook with her.

CHAPTER 5
Cooking Lessons

On Saturday, I'm finishing lunch. *Where are you really from?* Mrs. Smith's question, her tone, her look still bother me.

"Anne, did you hear me?" Mom asks as she clears dishes.

"Pardon me, Mom?"

"After yoga, I'll pick up a pizza and pick up

Elizabeth from Rohan's house. Help Jacob with his reading. Finish your homework," she says.

"Yes, Mom," I reply.

"Be good. Dad's in his office but don't disturb him unless it's important," she says before she leaves.

I know.

Dad works all the time. He's a lawyer and helps people come to Canada. It's the Vietnamese way that, as the eldest daughter, I care for my younger siblings. Like Auntie Hai does.

I take out Grandma Nội's jade bangle. I slip it on and feel the rushing wind around me.

"Precious granddaughter, will you help keep the harmony with the ancestors?" Grandma Nội asks.

"Yes," I say. She makes me feel safe. I want to tell her about ballet.

She smiles. "Good. I miss having đồ chua. Wash the carrots. And the daikon. Cut them like sticks," she directs me in her firm voice.

"Like fries!" I'm very slow, trying not to cut my finger.

"What? Talking to me?" Jacob asks from the kitchen table, looking up from his drawings.

"No, to Grandma Nội," I reply.

He tilts his head slightly. "I thought we only said prayers to her every new moon?"

I always tell Liz to watch out around Jacob. He notices everything.

"You can talk to her whenever you want," I say.

He thinks about it. "Okay." And goes back to drawing.

"Make a mix of water, vinegar, and sugar," Grandma Nội continues.

First, I mistake salt for sugar. Then I lose count measuring the vinegar. Finally, I'm ready to add the vegetables to the bowl.

"After, pack the vegetables tightly in a glass jar," she says.

Dad comes into the kitchen and grabs a banana. "Pickled vegetables? I love these. How do you know to make this dish?" he asks.

Grandma Nội's right beside me but I guess he doesn't know she's there. Grandma did say what was between her and other family members isn't for me to know. Just like her cooking lessons are between us.

"Grandma Nội," I answer.

"When I was your age, she worked at the sewing factory during the day and at the nail salon at night. She cooked before I woke up so I never cooked with her." He leaves.

"Your dad's job was to study. There was a lot we had to do when we first came to this country." Grandma Nội's voice is sad.

I take a deep breath. "Grandma, did people ever ask you where you were from?"

She snorts. "All the time! People would yell at me to go back to where I came from. They would shout things like *ching chong bing bang*. And people would pull their eyes into slits at me."

"That's so mean, Grandma," I say, feeling like I want to throw up.

What happened to Grandma Nội was much worse than what Mrs. Smith said to me. I guess I'm being too sensitive.

CHAPTER 6

What It Means to Be Vietnamese

At school, I stare at my multiplication worksheet. I can't concentrate.

At yesterday's ballet class, Mrs. Smith said to me, "You're such a good Asian girl. Girls like you never give me any trouble."

I asked Sophie about it after and she said, "She

paid you a compliment! You're so lucky!"

I didn't feel that way. How did Sophie see it so differently?

The recess bell rings.

"Anne, is everything okay? You seem distracted lately," my teacher, Ms. Singh, asks as I get ready to go out.

I want to tell her about Mrs. Smith. Then I feel silly. "I'm okay," I reply.

As I head outside, I start to think about Mark, my classmate last year. He said of course I got 100 percent on my math test. He said I'm Asian and Asians are good at math.

I think about when I had dinner at Sophie's house. Her mom asked me how we cook rice

on the stovetop. I told her we always used a rice cooker. That was the first time I understood not all families had rice cookers. I was the different one. My experiences were not the normal experiences.

It's only October but I have to wear my winter jacket already. I hope it doesn't snow before Halloween again this year. I see Jennifer laughing with some girls on the swings.

"Hey, Anne!" Serena, Jennifer's friend, waves me over. I head the other way, pretending not to hear her.

I sit by myself and think about what it means to be Vietnamese. I've never really thought about this stuff before. I wring my hands, feeling more and more uncertain.

Mom named all of us after characters from her favorite Canadian books. My sister's name is from *The Paper Bag Princess*. My brother's name is from *Jacob Two-Two Meets the Hooded Fang*. And I am Anne with an *E*, Anne Shirley from *Anne of Green Gables*. I always felt connected to Anne because I am good in school like she was. But now I feel out of place like she did when she first got to Green Gables.

Hao and Liz want to play tag.

"Come on, Anne," Liz calls out. "You're being boring," my sister jokes.

"Leave me alone!" I shout, and they back off. Liz looks so hurt. Yelling at her is the worst thing I could do to her. I feel bad but can't take it back now. I shake my head to try to clear out the jumble of thoughts and feelings. It doesn't work.

My cousins Hanh and Hao go to Vietnamese school every weekend. Liz and I go to ballet and Jacob goes to hockey. They've been to Vietnam on vacation. I've never been. We go to Mexico on vacation. Hanh and Hao bring sticky rice for lunch. We bring sandwiches.

I'm Vietnamese but I'm even different from my cousins.

Why does Mrs. Smith keep pointing me out? Is something wrong with me? Who am I?

CHAPTER 7
Making Bánh Xèo

It's the middle of November, about a month since Grandma Nội and I started cooking together, and I love it. When I put on the green jade bangle and we are together, I don't think of Mrs. Smith or any worries.

I do find cooking super tricky. I keep making mistakes and I hate making mistakes. Once, I overcooked the bún noodles and they fell apart into a big mess. Then I broke the eggs before we could hard boil them for the thịt kho.

This Sunday we are making bánh xèo, fold-over thin pancakes, with shrimp and pork.

"That's too much coconut milk," Grandma Nội says gently, pointing at the batter.

"Sorry," I say. "I'll do it over."

Jacob comes into the kitchen.

"How's your comic book?" I hug him. Liz is out helping Auntie Hai at the nail salon again.

"Good. What are we making?" he asks.

I smile and stir the batter carefully. "Just watch. Like this."

Jacob nods and copies me. He knows I don't

want a mess, but he stirs with all his strength and the batter goes everywhere. "I'm so good at this!"

Grandma Nội laughs. "Now heat the pan. Add the onions and meat. Now add the batter."

My pancakes keep sticking and burning.

"I messed it up again. I can't do this." I'm close to tears. I want to please the ancestors.

"Precious granddaughter, when I was your age, I had to make rice for the family. I cooked it on a pot over an open fire. Sometimes it was crunchy. Sometimes it was soup." She shakes her head. "I couldn't give up or we would not have anything to eat." She laughs and the sound fills the room.

"I'll still eat it," Jacob says.

I smile. "I want to make this for the next new moon and offer it to the ancestors."

"The family will have good fortune then," Grandma Nội replies.

Mom comes downstairs after her shower. "Bánh xèo? I ate that as a kid. Another one of Bà Nội's recipes?"

I nod. "I feel closer to her when I cook."

"Then you should keep cooking," Mom says as she strokes my hair.

"I helped too," Jacob adds.

Mom laughs. "My sisters and I always fought over who had to wash the herbs. No one liked that job. Somehow, I always ended up doing it, being the youngest in the family."

Cooking days are also super fun because Mom and Dad tell me things about their lives I've never heard before.

Mom asks me, "How was ballet class this week?"

"Good," I reply.

"Has the teacher talked about any solos yet?" she asks.

"Not yet," I say.

"It's still early. Work hard. Be respectful in class," she reminds me.

The butterflies in my tummy that disappear when I cook are back again. I only forget for a short time.

"I love watching you dance. Our parents left

our homeland, after the war, to give us all a better life in Canada," Mom continues. "I always wanted to be a prima ballerina."

I nod. I've heard this before. I'll make Mom proud of me.

CHAPTER 8

In a Bad Mood

From the moment Mrs. Smith enters the studio, I can tell she is in a bad mood. Her arms are crossed over her chest and her lips are scrunched together.

"Sophie!" she yells. "That chassé was sloppy. Be light on your feet. We are ballerinas not elephants!"

Sophie's face turns bright red.

Mrs. Smith turns to Jennifer. "Higher, higher

on your passé." She points to Jennifer's foot. "Make sure it's above the knee or why even bother?"

Jennifer looks down.

My shoulders tense. I don't want Mrs. Smith to pay attention to me.

"Anne, keep time with the others!" she shouts.

I try to imitate the other girls around me.

"Anne, I'm speaking English. Do you understand? Keep up!" she says quickly.

I'm breathing heavily now.

"Stop! Everyone watch Anne do her demi-plié," Mrs. Smith says.

All eyes fall on me and my heart beats faster.

"You people are usually very flexible. Girls like you can squat for long hours. I would think your

demi-plié would be much better. Make sure to send your knees directly out over your toes!" She moves on.

My cheeks are flaming red. I'm hot and try to hold back the tears, wishing I could just turn invisible.

At the end of class, Mrs. Smith calls out, "Remember, girls, for the last class before winter break, bring in a holiday dish to share. No nuts."

Sophie has to leave right after class. Jennifer comes to talk to me as we both wait to be picked up.

"You okay? Mrs. Smith was mean," she says.

Jennifer being nice to me surprises me. It takes me a moment to react.

"She's tough on all of us. She keeps saying it'll make us stronger," I reply. But it's what she says to me . . . *you people* . . .

Jennifer shakes her head. "Sure. But she always points out how different you are."

I'm shocked. How does Jennifer notice when Sophie, my good friend, doesn't? "She's the teacher. What can I do?"

Jennifer leans on me a little. "I always thought everything was easy for you." She shrugs. "Maybe not everything."

We're both silent.

"She makes me feel like I don't belong," I whisper.

Jennifer snorts. "Of course you do! We've been in all the same ballet classes since kindergarten. Like what would I do if you weren't there? What would it matter if I got a solo if I didn't beat you?"

I actually smile. "Oh, I'll get the solo, don't worry," I say back.

We both laugh.

CHAPTER 9
What's Wrong with Me?

One Friday evening in December, Liz and I are watching TV in the living room. Jacob is over at Grandpa Nội's house watching the Jets hockey game with him.

"What if me and Rohan tell our parents we have to do Taekwondo because it's good for our health?" Liz wonders.

"Still trying to get Mom to let you quit ballet?" I respond as I fold laundry.

Liz says, "I don't love it like you do."

Not anymore. The butterflies in my tummy have turned into rocks, always there. I'm not able to sleep. I'm not hungry anymore. But if I get a solo and make Mom happy, everything will be fine.

"Cards? Or video games?" Liz's face is bright with hope.

"Can't. I want to get ingredients ready to try a new recipe tomorrow," I say.

I also love cooking with Grandma Nội because every time she tells me a different story about my ancestors. Once when we made gỏi cuốn rice paper rolls, she said, "Before the soldiers came and we had to move, my fourth sister, Chị Tư, and I would ride our bikes up and down the lane, wearing our áo dài tunics." Another time, when we made gỏi xoài mango salad, she said, "My sixth aunt, Dì Sáu, was the dancer in the family. She danced the most beautiful lantern dance for Mid-Autumn Festival. You are like her."

Liz rolls her eyes. "Ugh, again? That's all you do now, cook! So boring." She laughs.

If she only knew what I was going through. I think briefly about telling Liz but instead I snap. "At least it's something useful. Not like you, thinking of dumb ideas to get your way."

Her eyes start to tear up. "You suck. You don't care about anyone but yourself." She runs upstairs.

I feel bad. What's wrong with me?

Before I can go after Liz, Dad says, "Anne, come here." He waves at me to follow him to his office at the front of the house.

Mom is already waiting there.

Oh no, this is super bad.

"We just looked at your report card on the school portal," Dad says.

My tests and assignments have been poor.

"You got some *meets expectations* and some *below expectations*. No exceeds expectations." Dad's voice is gentle. "This is not what we expect from you."

Mom continues, "Your teacher writes how you are not listening, not participating, not

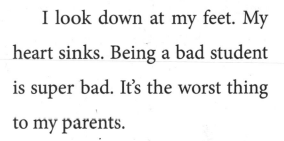

concentrating." Her voice is not gentle.

I look down at my feet. My heart sinks. Being a bad student is super bad. It's the worst thing to my parents.

"What's going on, Anne?" Dad asks.

I shrug.

"Your language arts marks are poor. Your math marks are even worse. This isn't like you," Mom says, speaking loudly.

I should be sad. Instead, I'm angry. I snap again and spit out, "Why? Is it because Asian people are supposed to be good at math?"

Mom gasps. And Dad just looks tired.

I look down again. I have never yelled at my parents like that.

Dad speaks first. "No, because you are good at math. You are a good student."

"And you are respectful and you are kind," Mom adds.

"Anne, is there anything you want to tell us?" Dad asks.

I don't know what to say. My anger is replaced with guilt for disappointing them. I am so mixed up. I shake my head.

CHAPTER 10

Everyone Loves Spring Rolls

"I'm so stupid. Dad and Mom hate me. Liz won't talk to me. Sophie doesn't get me. Everything's bad." I'm lying on my bed while playing with the green jade bangle. Grandma Nội shimmers beside me.

"Precious granddaughter, your mom and dad

love you. Promise them you will work harder to raise your marks. You will feel better if we cook something. What do you want to bring to ballet?" Grandma Nội says.

"It's a holiday party, so holiday foods. Something everyone likes." I smile. "Chả giò. Everyone loves spring rolls. Always at parties, they're gone quickly. They're Grandpa Nội's favourite. Even Jacob eats a ton," I say, sitting up now.

"Chả giò it is. Apologize to your parents for being disrespectful. Then ask them to buy the ingredients."

The day before the ballet holiday party, it's snowing hard and there is a wind-chill warning. Liz is avoiding me and got Jacob to side with her. That hurt.

"Mix the filling of ground pork, noodles, carrots, and mushrooms," Grandma Nội instructs.

I lay out the square spring roll wrapper so it looks like a diamond.

"Now add a spoonful of filling near the bottom in the shape of a log," Grandma Nội says. Pull the bottom corner of the wrapper over the filling. Roll to the middle. Fold in one side and then the other side. Then roll up the whole thing, tight and round."

My first ten rolls look sloppy. I stomp my feet, so mad at myself. These have to be perfect. For

Mrs. Smith to like me. For Mom to be proud. For the ancestors to grant us good fortune. For everything to be better.

"Anne, don't give up. We are making chả giò the same way I made them with my mother and she made them with her parent. A long line of our ancestors," Grandma Nội says. "I broke that line with your dad but am fixing it now. You are our future."

I cry suddenly. All the pressure inside me bursts out.

"What's wrong, precious granddaughter?" Grandma Nội asks.

"But I don't know who I am," I sob. "How can I be the future?"

"You are our hope in this country. You are our dream woven together by breath and blood. All of your ancestors are in you, Anne." I feel her hand over my chest, over my heart. It makes me feel strong.

"I miss you," I whisper.

"I am with you always. Who are you?" Grandma Nội asks.

"I am Anne Nguyen," I say.

Even though I'm still wearing the green jade bangle, Grandma

Nội begins to shimmer softly. I no longer need her in the same way I did before. She disappears into darkness.

CHAPTER 11
Holiday Party

At the holiday party, we lay out all our dishes on a table at the back of the dance studio. I hope Mrs. Smith can see I worked as hard on the chả giò as I work in class. I picked out the 30 best rolls to serve today. I also brought nước mắm fish sauce for dipping.

"I love spring rolls, Anne!" Sophie says beside

me as she lays out meatballs.

Jennifer comes up on the other side of me. "Looks yummy." She uncovers colorful sugar cookies in the shape of stars, Christmas trees, and mittens.

"Thanks. Your cookies look great," I reply.

Mrs. Smith comes in with a big grin on her face. "Hello, girls. Smells very good in here." She's holding paper plates and napkins. She sets them down and starts looking at the food.

"Who brought the cookies? Jennifer, nice! Turkey. Yum, Laura! Fried mashed potato balls. So creative, Emily! And . . ." She stops.

Mrs. Smith points at the chả giò.

"I made them," I say proudly.

Her eyes widen. "Spring rolls? Oh darling, I was thinking of normal foods for the party." She chuckles, a low laugh that comes deep from her belly.

I look at the table. Sugar cookies. Meatballs. What I think is cranberry jelly. Sliced turkey with gravy. Stuffing in muffin tins. Cheese and crackers. There is one plate that doesn't belong. Mine.

I'm so embarrassed. Again, I'm reminded I'm different. I'm not in step with everyone else. My cheeks are on fire and my hands are so sweaty.

Everyone stops. Sophie looks nervous and backs away from me. The other girls are quiet.

"It's okay. I'm sure it's good." Mrs. Smith

wrinkles her nose. "Just cover up the sauce, please. It's very strong."

My heart races and my chest tightens. My lips quiver and tears start to form at the corners of my eyes.

I touch the green jade bangle I'm wearing. It's cool and soothing. I think of Grandma Nội and what I learned from her. *I am Anne Nguyen.*

I stand a bit taller. I breathe out. It wasn't a mistake bringing the spring rolls. I'm proud of my Vietnamese heritage. And I'm not going to change for Mrs. Smith or for anyone.

The tears don't come. My heart is still beating fast but now I feel alert. I feel ready to stand up to her.

"Mrs. Smith, this is what I eat for the holidays. And I'm proud of that," I say, and I walk out of class.

CHAPTER 12
Something Isn't Right

I hide along the side of the building until Mom comes to get me. She can tell something isn't right, but she'll wait to talk to me with Dad there.

At home that night, they both come into my bedroom.

"The dance school called and said there was a

misunderstanding. Mrs. Smith wants to know if you're okay," Dad says.

"I don't know what's going on with you lately. Poor grades. Walking out of ballet," Mom says more loudly.

"What's wrong, Anne? Tell us," Dad says.

I think of Grandma Nội's words. *All the ancestors are in me.*

I take a deep breath. "Mrs. Smith. She seems nice but I don't like what she says to me. She keeps pointing out how different I am. It makes me feel less than other people."

My parents look at each other, their eyes wide. Something clicks. They seem to get it.

"Tell us everything she said," Mom says, so

softly that I feel confident to continue.

As I share with my parents, the knots in my stomach start to uncurl.

Mom hugs me, which surprises me. "Anne, what she said to you is not okay. Those comments were racist. And we will not accept it."

"I'm sorry I won't get the solo. I'm sorry to disappoint you," I say quickly.

"I don't care about that," Mom replies.

"What do you want to do about ballet?" Dad asks.

"Can we tell the dance school about what I told you?" I ask.

"Yes, we can make a complaint to the school," Dad replies.

"And I don't want to go back to Mrs. Smith's class," I say.

Before I fall asleep that night, I feel Grandma Nội's hands on my face. Even though the jade bangle is in its red box on my dresser, I know she is with me.

At school the next day, Jennifer walks over to me at recess. Hao and I are building a snow castle.

"Hey," I say.

"Hey. So what happened yesterday?" she asks.

"I talked to my parents. We're going to make a complaint about Mrs. Smith," I respond.

"I wanted to say something. But I didn't know how," she says.

I nod. "It's hard. She's a teacher."

"I'll tell my parents I want to make a complaint too," she adds.

"What about a solo? She didn't treat you that way."

"Last year, you stood up for me when Emma teased me about my two dads. We weren't friends. I can stand up for you now. Like friends." She starts helping with the castle.

"Definitely friends," I reply.

CHAPTER 13

Our Ancestors Are in Us

The new year brings a glittering snowstorm. It makes me think of Anne of Green Gables when she talks about tomorrow being a new day without any mistakes in it.

Jennifer, Sophie, and I have started at a new dance school and we have just finished our first class.

Sophie zips up her jacket. "Miss Wang is really nice." She pauses. "Do you think so too, Anne?"

I nod and smile. After feeling so bad about what happened with Mrs. Smith, Sophie is trying hard to ask me what I think.

"See you next time, besties!" Jennifer calls out as she leaves, and we wave to her.

I spot my parents' car in the parking lot and Dad is behind the wheel. "Why are you picking me up? Don't you have to work?" I get in and turn up the heat.

"I'm working less. Let me show you something," he replies.

We drive to The Forks downtown and get out. It's strange. It's never just me and Dad. He leads me

past the market and restaurants to the river trail.

"Everything okay in class?" Dad asks.

I nod. Dad and Mom are also trying super hard to know what is going on with me. They ask me how I am now . . . a lot.

Dad looks out at the river. "When I was a kid, watching the skaters here, I wanted to be like them, to play hockey, to fit in. I wanted to be a normal Canadian kid. Not a poor immigrant weird kid," he says. "A group of boys saw me staring at them and called me racist names and threw snowballs at me."

I don't know what to say. Dad never talks like this.

He keeps going. "All I wanted for you, for all of

you, was what I didn't have growing up. I thought if Mom and I didn't talk about all the bad things, and about where we came from, it would be better for you and your sister and brother growing up."

"But I need to know what to do when people are being racist. I need to know about the bad things. And to discover more Vietnamese stuff," I say. "And who I am," I add in a whisper.

Dad nods. "I'm proud of you for standing up for yourself. You can always talk to me, about anything, con yêu quý, precious daughter."

"Grandma Nội used to call me precious granddaughter."

I see how Dad looks like Grandma Nội. The nose is the same. And it's my nose too. I hear

Grandma Nội's voice in my dad's big laugh. Our ancestors are in us.

"I need to learn more too. About Vietnamese stuff," Dad adds.

"It's okay. Let's learn together," I reply.

Even though it's super cold, I'm warm on the inside as Dad and I hold hands, as the snow swirls around us.

CHAPTER 14
Family Spirits

It's new moon day in January. Next month's new moon day will be Tết, the Lunar New Year. Today, I'm in charge of making food offerings for Grandma Nội and all the ancestors. It's a family activity now.

School has been super good this term. I am actually good at math! Dad, Liz, and I are all

learning Vietnamese with a tutor once a week. Liz is the quickest learner, and she loves that! I'm also relieved we made up.

"Dad, can you wash the herbs and lettuce?" I ask as I make bánh xèo, not burning the pancakes this time.

"No one likes that job," he says sadly. "Can your mom do it?"

"I'm busy rolling the chả giò with Elizabeth and Jacob," Mom replies.

We all laugh at Dad as he plucks the herbs.

Auntie and Uncle Hai, Hanh and Hao, and Grandpa Nội come over for dinner. They bring pomelo fruit and grass jelly chè for dessert.

We have more đồ chua I pickled last month. We

also have bún noodles and pan-fried sliced beef. Hao and Liz set out all the plates on the altar and I rearrange them. I still like to make sure the chopsticks are perfectly set next to the bowls of rice.

Dad lights the joss sticks and passes them around. We all say our prayers. We all have our own private moments with the family spirits.

I feel Grandma Nội in the room—a gentle weight on my shoulders and soft hands on my face. I do wear the green jade bangle sometimes,

but I don't need it to feel her with me. After all, I believe in ghosts.

We sit down together for dinner after all the incense burns away and the ancestors have shared in the meal.

"Ngon quá," Grandpa Nội exclaims, saying the food is so tasty.

"I helped," Jacob mentions. "These chả giò are mine." He points to a pile of rolls, some fat, some long, some square.

"I see that. Very nice," says Uncle Hai, smiling at me.

Hao says, "Hey, Anne, can you teach me how to make đồ chua?" He's eating them with his chopsticks like he hasn't eaten all day.

"How about you master toast for breakfast first?" Hanh teases him.

"I want this for breakfast instead," Hao replies.

"Used to have phở for breakfast in Vietnam," Auntie Hai says.

"I did too, growing up here," Mom adds.

"I like doughnuts better for breakfast," Liz replies.

We all laugh.

As I look around at the circle of my family, I know the ghosts of my ancestors do grant us good fortune. Mixed in with all the voices of my family, I can hear Grandma Nội's big laugh too.

All About Anne and Her Family

Anne Nguyen is nine years old and she's in grade four. She organizes all her stuffies by the colors of the rainbow. Her favorite thing about winter in Winnipeg is how fresh snow on trees looks super sparkly.

Liz Nguyen is seven years old and she's in grade two. She loves movies with superheroes because they have cool powers and everyone cheers for them. She thinks it's awesome how in the winter, she gets hot chocolate with whipped cream and marshmallows after playing outside— sooo yummy!

Jacob Nguyen is six years old and he's in grade one. He wants to draw pictures for books when he grows up. He can't wait for winter so he can skate outside at the community center, feeling like he's flying on the ice.

Mom works with computers in a tall building downtown. Her happy place is at the gym, especially the hot yoga studio. Her idea of a fun vacation is being near water and not having to cook all the time.

Dad is a lawyer who helps people from all over the world come to Canada. His favorite foods are any kind of noodles and sauce, yum! He's never had a dog before and has always wanted a black Lab.

Cousin Hanh is fifteen years old and she's in grade ten. She loves reading fantasy novels and writes different endings to books in her journal. Winter for her is all about the cute boots and fancy scarves she wears to express herself.

Cousin Hao is nine years old and he's in grade four. He collects rocks and really wants a moon rock. He has the best time in winter after a snowstorm, when he can build a snow fort complete with a corner to store snowballs.

Grandma Nội is the best cook and she would sometimes eat dessert first before eating dinner. She collected figurines of the Vietnamese zodiac and áo dài fabric. She used to tell a lot of stories about the family and Vietnamese fairy tales.

Grandpa Nội likes to grow flowers, fruits, and vegetables. He misses the feeling of the open, blue sky like when he lived on a farm in Vietnam. He can't wait for hockey playoffs every year.

Auntie Hai works at a nail salon painting people's nails. Her favorite color is red: a lucky color. She writes poetry in Vietnamese about love and family.

Uncle Hai's job is helping care for people at the hospital. His goal is to take his family back to Vietnam on vacation every three years. He likes taking pictures around the neighborhood and at the Buddhist temple.

Author's Note

I hope you've had a great time hanging out with Anne and her family. For this book, I thought about what it may feel like to not quite belong, what being a good friend may mean, and what it could be like to walk in someone else's shoes. This is my offering.

Having altars to the ancestors is a Vietnamese custom I grew up with after my dad passed away when I was seven years old, younger than Anne is in this book. We made offerings of food and recognized death anniversaries. I have prayed to my dad and have felt his presence around me. You may have your own special ways to remember loved ones.

A note about the language in this series: sometimes the Vietnamese words are spelled in Vietnamese with accents, and they are pronounced in Vietnamese. And sometimes the Vietnamese words have no accents and are pronounced in a way that fits with how words are pronounced in English. I've made these choices based on how I imagined the character would say them/think of them.

For example, Nguyen as a last name is written as Nguyễn in Vietnamese. I have chosen to write it as Nguyen without the accents as I imagine the siblings would write it like that at school and pronounce their last name in an English way. Yet for most food like chả giò, I've added accents as I imagine them saying the words in Vietnamese.

Also, sometimes I have chosen to merge English and Vietnamese words. In Vietnamese, a person would call their dad's mom Bà Nội and their dad's dad Ông Nội. I have merged Grandma and Grandpa with Nội. A person would call their dad's oldest sister Cô Hai and call their dad's oldest sister's husband Dượng Hai. I merged Auntie and Uncle with Hai. I imagine this is a decision Anne's family made. It may be different with each family.

Thank you so much for choosing this book. Feel free to reach out to me at lindaytrinh.com. Take care!

Linda

Acknowledgments

Much gratitude to the entire team at Annick Press for believing in and supporting The Nguyen Kids series and this book, my first book baby. Thanks to Katie for being such a careful and responsive editor; it means so much to me that we could talk through anything. Thanks to Kaela, Jieun, Eleanor, and Mary Ann for their insights. Thanks to Clayton for his amazing illustrations.

Love to all my extended family and friends for their support and thanks to those who read various drafts. Thanks to fellow author Jodi for reading the first draft and offering invaluable feedback and mentorship. Thanks to my best friend Mirna for our long conversations about young readers and for always being there for me. Thanks to my cousins Ky and Bao for their perspectives and encouragement. Thanks to my big sister Jen, my biggest fangirl, for loving all my words and helping me explore our Vietnamese heritage. Thanks to my husband, Ryan, for giving me the space and support to take the chance on myself to be an author.

Thanks to my kids, Lexi and Evan, who inspire me with their curiosity, bravery, kindness, and perseverance. Lexi was my first reader and offered great insights and Evan had great ideas for me. I'm so humbled that they're able to see kids like themselves in this series. Mama loves you! And of course, thanks to my mom for making this life possible for me, and for showing me every day what hard work looked like when I was growing up. Also, for always cooking for me with love, and now for her cháu ngoại.

I'll be forever grateful to my dad, my grandparents, and to all my ancestors for everything they have sacrificed and accomplished so that I may live out my dreams.

THE NGUYEN KIDS
The Power of the
PEARL EARRINGS
written by
Linda Trinh
illustrated by
Clayton Nguyen

CHAPTER 1

I'm the Leader!

"Now what, Liz?" Rohan, Best Friend Ever, asks me. He grabs a handful of ketchup chips.

I shrug. We're hanging out in my living room. It's the Sunday before school starts and it's raining. It's so boring being trapped inside.

"Let's play Trung Warriors!" I stand up quickly. "To practice for our first Taekwondo class."

"Okay!" Rohan says as he leaps onto the couch.

"You were Trưng Trắc last time. I'm the leader!" I move to stand in front of him. "I'm at the front of the elephant. You're my sister, Trưng Nhị."

My Grandma Nội used to babysit me and Rohan. My grandma used to tell us the story of Hai Bà Trưng, two brave sisters who lived a long time ago. They were warriors, great fighters, and fought for freedom. They were Vietnamese like I am.

"The invaders are coming!" I shout and pull out my imaginary sword.

Rohan pulls out his imaginary sword too. We jump from our elephant to fight the bad guys.

I get my short hair stuck on one of my pearl

earrings when I do a spin kick move. The pearl earrings were a gift from Grandma Nội. My sister got our grandma's jade bangle. And my brother got her painted fan. My gift is the coolest.

I look over at Grandma Nội's picture on her altar in our dining room. She died over a year ago now. Dad and Mom say we Vietnamese believe the spirits of our family, our ancestors, stay with us after they pass away. They hear our prayers. They watch out for us. I hope she's happy I'm wearing her earrings.

"The other fighters are too strong! To the river," Rohan says, just like we've played so many times. He runs to the window.

I jab and duck and fight my way over to him.

We are back-to-back as we swing our invisible swords around. I throw cushions and pillows everywhere.

Me and Rohan lie on the floor after the battle.

That's how my older sister, Miss Perfect, Anne, finds me. Dad and Mom are always busy with her and my younger brother, The Baby, Jacob. I get lost in the middle most of the time.

Dad always said it's Anne's job as the oldest sister to look after us. She's only two years older than me. I'm eight, but she thinks she's the boss of me.

"Hey, we have to practice," Anne says.

My boring sister and her boring ballet friends, Sophie and Jennifer, want to wreck my fun, again.

"We were here first. Basement?" I reply.

"The floor here is better. You go to the basement!" she says.

"Mom!" we yell at the same time.

Mom comes in from the kitchen. "Liz, Rohan, please! The girls have a performance." She gives me that look—*don't make trouble.*

"My mom always sides with Anne," I say as

Rohan and I head down the basement stairs. I stomp my feet.

"At least she let you quit ballet," Rohan replies.

It's true. Before Anne changed ballet schools, Mom would never have let me. Now she asks questions about how I'm feeling and if things bother me. But there's one thing that hasn't changed. She still sides with my sister!

Rohan punches in the air. "And now we'll both be in Mrs. Goodman's grade three class and take Taekwondo together!"

I nod, happy again. "We can be like the Trung Warriors for real!" I say, kicking into the air.

About the Author

Linda Trinh is a Vietnamese Canadian author who writes stories for kids and grown-ups. Like Anne, she believes in ghosts. She believes her ancestors are still with her, especially her dad who passed away when she was little. That makes her feel connected to her past and hopeful for the future. Unlike Anne, she *still* finds cooking super tricky and is more likely to order phở beef noodle soup from her favorite restaurant than to make it herself. She spends a lot of time staring out her window, daydreaming, and pacing around the house, writing in her head way before she types out anything. She lives with her husband and two kids in Winnipeg.

About the Illustrator

Clayton Nguyen is an artist working on animated TV shows and films to bring imaginary characters and worlds to life. In a complete coincidence, Clayton also started drawing at an early age and has two older sisters, just like Jacob. Being the youngest sibling, he is still sometimes treated like the baby of the family. Some of his earliest memories of becoming interested in art come from watching TV shows like *Art Attack* and anime with his sisters after school. Nowadays, when he isn't drawing, you'll often find him playing video games or getting bubble tea in Toronto.

Look for Book 3 in the Nguyen Kids series, coming soon!

THE NGUYEN KIDS

The Mystery of the PAINTED FAN

written by
Linda Trinh

illustrated by
Clayton Nguyen